Dear Beast

by DORI HILLESTAD BUTLER

illustrated by
KEVAN ATTEBERRY

HOLIDAY HOUSE • NEW YORK

For Andy. And Simon. (Best grandkitty ever!)—D.H.B.

For my letter-writing friends. And the USPS for making the magic happen.—K.A.

Text copyright © 2020 by Dori Hillestad Butler   Illustrations copyright © 2020 by Kevan Atteberry

All Rights Reserved   HOLIDAY HOUSE is registered in the U.S. Patent and Trademark Office.

Printed and bound in January 2020 at Tien Wah Press, Johor Bahru, Johor, Malaysia.   The artwork was created digitally with Photoshop.

www.holidayhouse.com   First Edition   1 3 5 7 9 10 8 6 4 2

Library of Congress Cataloging–in–Publication Data   Names: Butler, Dori Hillestad, author. | Atteberry, Kevan, illustrator.

Title: Dear Beast / by Dori Hillestad Butler ; illustrated by Kevan Atteberry.   Description: First edition. | New York : Holiday House, [2020]

Series: Dear Beast ; #1 | Audience: Ages 5–8 | Audience: Grades 2–3 | Summary: Through a series of letters, Simon, a grumpy and jealous cat, informs

Baxter, his boy's new dog, that he is not welcome and should leave at once.   Identifiers: LCCN 2019022779 | ISBN 9780823444922 (hardcover)

Subjects: CYAC: Cats—Fiction. | Dogs—Fiction. | Letters—Fiction. | Humorous stories.   Classification: LCC PZ7.B9759 De 2020 | DDC [Fic]—dc23

LC record available at https://lccn.loc.gov/2019022779

CONTENTS

4

ONE
NOT NEEDED

FROM THE DESK OF

Simon

Dear Dog,
It has come to my attention that you wish to care for my boy, Andy. This letter is to inform you that your services are not needed. I've been with Andy and his family for many years. I prefer to care for him on my own. Please find yourself another human. There are many in need of a pet. Thank you for your interest.

Sincerely,
SIMON

FROM THE DESK OF

Simon

Dear Dog,

What do you mean, no can do? Perhaps you misunderstand the situation.

Yes, Andy has two homes now. It's too bad his parents no longer live together.

However, Andy does not need another pet. Please check yourself in to the nearest animal shelter. You'll have an opportunity to meet many fine humans while you're there. Take your time and choose the one that's right for you.

Thank you.

Sincerely,
SIMON

I alreddy did. I picked Andy! And he picked me! YAY!!!

FROM THE DESK OF
Simon

Dear Dog,

   Don't you know how to write a proper letter? I can forgive your lack of a date, address, and return address. But you didn't even include a salutation, closing, or signature.

   Also, please check your spelling. It's A–L–R–E–A–D–Y, not A–L–R–E–D–D–Y. Would you like to see it spelled correctly in a sentence? "ANDY ALREADY HAS A PET!" Two pets if you count Bubbles.

   Please be on your way.

Sincerely,
SIMON

Fine. I'll rite you a proper letter.
Deer Siman. Give me a brake.
I'm wurking on my speling. Speling
is hard! By the way, you can call me
Baxter. That's my name. You noe
whut thay say. When a hyooman
gives you a name, you get to
stay!!!! Yay!!!!

From, Baxter

TWO
LET'S BE FRENDS!

FROM THE DESK OF
Simon

Dear Dog,

I prefer to call you Dog. Or perhaps I'll call you Beast. Aren't you embarrassed by yourself, Beast?

Furthermore, Andy now has the sniffles. He could be allergic to you. If he is, you can't stay. I'm sorry to be the bearer of bad news.

Sincerely,

SIMON (Please note it's O–N, not A–N)

Deer Siman,

Why wood I be imbarrassed by myself?

It's nice that you want to give me a nick name. That meens you like me. YAY! But I'm not much of a beest. See? Here's a pickchur to prove it. And don't wurry. I get to stay! Andy's dad adoptid me. Did you noe Andy and his dad always wantid a dog? But Andy's mom sed no. Cuz she's a cat purson. Lucky YOU!!!

Andy's dad sez I will be good for Andy. I'll teach him ree-spon-su-bill-it-ee. And I'll be his frend at his dad's howse. Andy needs more frends. He's reelly shy you noe.

Luv,

Baxter

FTS: You noe whut thay say. A dog for evry child and a child for evry dog!

16

FROM THE DESK OF
Simon

Dear Beast,

No one says that!

Furthermore, you may have been adopted, but there's a trial period. Andy's father can still send you back. Or you can choose to leave. Please make a good choice.

Finally, it's P.S., not F.T.S. Why in the world would you think it's F.T.S.? P.S. is short for "post scriptum." It's Latin. It means "written after." P.S. can also be short for "Please Scram."

Sincerely,
SIMON (not SIMAN)

Deer Simmon,

I did not noe that abowt PS. That's very intresting. FTS is short for Fergot To Say. I don't speek Latin so if you don't mind I'll keep yoozing FTS. It makes more sens than PS. Don't you think?

Luv and Liver Treets,
Baxter

FTS: LET'S BE FRENDS!!!!!!!!

FROM THE DESK OF
Simon

Dear Beast,
  I regret to inform you that we cannot be friends.

Sincerely,
SIMON

THREE
ANDY'S SNIFFLES

FROM THE DESK OF
Simon

Dear Beast,

Andy's sniffles have gotten worse. Furthermore, he is sneezing and coughing now, too. He is clearly allergic to you. Therefore, I really must insist you find another family. Andy's health depends upon it.

Seriously,
SIMON

Simun,

   Relax. Andy's just got a cold. No big
deel. He probly got it from his new frend
Noah. He was sneezing all over
the plase.

   Isn't it grate Andy has a new frend?
Noah lives next door. I saw Noah playing
owtside and I sed, Hay! Come meet my
boy Andy! And he did! And now thay're
frends! YAY!!!! Thay both like bord games
and video games.

   Noah calls Andy A Man. And Andy calls
Noah N Man. Then thay do a little danse.
Maybe you shud call me B Man. And I'll
call you S Man. Then we can do a danse
and be frends like Andy and Noah! YAY!!!!

Luv and Liver Treets,
The B Man

FROM THE DESK OF

Simon

Dear Beast,

I do not dance. Furthermore, I will not call you "B Man" and you may not call me "S Man." I already told you that we cannot be friends.

Andy's mother is taking him to the doctor this afternoon. As soon as she finds out about Andy's allergy, you will be gone, Beast! Do not let the door hit you on your way out.

Firmly,
SIMON

Deer Si Man,
   I told you! Andy has a cold! The docktur sed he will be better in a cupple days.
YAY!!!!

Okay. We don't have to be frends.
But we do have to figyor owt how to
share Andy. I bet yor good at stuff
like homewurk and chores. I'm good at
fun stuff like going owtside to play!
YAY! OWTSIDE!!! YAY! PLAY!!!!

So how abowt this? You make sure
Andy duz his wurk and I'll make sure
he has FUN!

Cool Drool?

The Bax Man

Simon

Dear Beast,

    DO NOT call me Si Man.

    DO NOT take Andy outside when he has a cold.

    For your information, he and I have all kinds of fun together indoors. We watch educational television. We sort his baseball cards. Sometimes we get wild and play Get the Dot.

    Andy is MY boy. We cannot share him!

Frustratedly,
SIMON

    P.S. There is nothing cool about drool.

F O U R
STINKY TO THE RESCUE

Deer Simun,

Good nooz! Andy is over his cold! YAY!!!!! But did you noe he can bearly thro a ball? He luvs baseball cards, but he can't thro a ball.

I get it. You don't like to go owtside so you never tawt him to play ball. And his parents are bizzy. But I luv to go owtside!!! YAY! OWTSIDE!!!! I'll teech him to play ball! No need to thank me. It's my pleshur.

See? This is why Andy needs BOTH of us.

Luv and Liver Treets,
Master Baxter Man

FTS: If you don't want to call me B Man or Bax Man, maybe you can call me Master Baxter Man? That's what Andy calls me sumtimes! YAY NICK NAMES!!!!

FROM THE DESK OF

Simon

Dear Beast,

Why would I thank you? Andy was supposed to work on his book report at his dad's house. But he didn't get anything done last night because he was too busy playing with you! You are a bad influence, Beast!

This is a warning. If you have not left by the end of this week, I will be forced to take serious action. Please don't make me do that.

For real,

S-I-M-O-N

Oh, Simen!

Andy's book reeport isn't doo till next week. He's got plenty of time.

There's more to life than book reeports, you noe. Like fun! YAY FUN!!!! A hyooman boy needs three owers of fun evry day! Did you noe that???

Luv and Liver Treets,
Master Baxter Man

Simon

Dear Stinky,

   We have a problem. A D-O-G now lives with my human's father. They're at 123 Lake Park Lane. I'm sure you're as unhappy about this as I am. I've tried to get him to leave, but nothing I've tried has worked. Would you care to try?

Hopefully yours,
SIMON

Dear Simon,

Oh no. Not another D-O-G. They're such busybodies. Always staring out the window and tattling to their humans.

I don't go looking for trouble in a dog's yard, you know. Most of the time, I'm just trying to get home to my kids. But as soon as a D-O-G sees you passing through, it's BARK! BARK! BARK! BARK! BARK! Gives me such a headache.

I'd trade my white stripe for the chance to walk safely and quietly through the backyard at 123 Lake Park Lane. I'll see if I can get rid of the D-O-G.

Yours truly,
STINKY

FIVE
WHY ANDY DIDN'T WRITE
HIS BOOK REPORT

Deer Simin,

Gess whut? I met yur frend Stinky yestrday. We played hide and seek. YAY! HIDE AND SEEK!!! But I don't think he undrstud the rools. I fownd him rite away. He didn't even try to run.

When I fownd him I sed, YOR IT! And you noe whut he did? He turned arownd, lifted his tail, and sprayed sumthing stinky

35

rite in my face!!!! I gess that's why you call him Stinky?

Enyway, Andy and his dad had to take me to the vet. I noe you noe that lady! She asked Andy how you were. He said you were grumpy and evrywon laffed!

Then the vet told me that I needed a bath with toematoe joose. And she gave me FIVE biskits. YAY! BISKITS!!! Do you get that many???

We had to go to the store for toematoe joose. When we got home, I got a reelly, reelly, reelly long bath owtside. Then I got anuther reelly, reelly, reelly long bath inside. And then I got towul time! YAY TOWUL TIME!!!!!!!!

It took a wile to do all that so gess whut? Andy didn't get his book reeport ritten! And it's doo tumorow.

I hope he du2n't get in trubble.

The good nooz is Andy spent lots of time owtside yestrday. YAY OWTSIDE!!! But I noe homewurk is importint, too. Maybe you shud teech Stinky how to play hide and seek so Andy can get his homewurk dun next time?

By the way, if you don't want to call me B Man or Master Baxter Man how abowt Just Plain Bax?

Luv and Liver Treets,
    Just Plain Bax. Or Bax.

FTS: Hay! This is the longest letter I have ritten in my whole intire life!

Simon

Dear Beast,

    You are a menace! An absolute menace!

                      Furiously,

                      SIMON

Deer Simin,

    Whut's a menace? And why are you so mad???

           Luv and Liver Treets,

           Bax

FROM THE DESK OF

Simon

Dear Stinky,
  What happened? I thought you were handling our problem?

Curiously yours,
SIMON

Dear Simon,
    I tried. Unfortunately, I think the
D-O-G is here to stay.
                        Yours truly,
                        STINKY

SIX

BLUB ... BLUB ...

FROM THE DESK OF

Simon

Dear Bubbles,

I am so glad we were able to put our little misunderstanding behind us. How are you? How is it living with Andy's dad?

I've heard that a wild beast has moved in. I'm so sorry. You must be as upset as I am.

I understand your options are limited as you cannot leave your bowl. Alas, I rarely leave my home as well. But there must be something we can do to get the beast to leave. Perhaps if we work together? Do you have any ideas?

I await your kind reply.

Sincerely yours,

SIMON

Dear Simon,

Misunderstanding??? *BLUB-BLUB-BLUB!!!*
You stuck your face in my bowl and tried
to eat me! *BLUB-BLUB-BLUB!!!*

But life is short. So I forgive you.
Breathe and forgive. *BLUB-blub* . . .
Breathe and forgive. *Blub* . . . *blub* . . .

I must admit I was worried when Baxter
came to live with us. *Blub* . . . *blub* . . . He
runs around the house like a maniac. And
he's a little on the clumsy side. *BLUB-Blub-
blub* . . .

I was afraid he might knock my bowl over.
But I don't think he can reach it. *Blub* . . .
blub . . . And the humans seem to like him.
Blub . . . *blub* . . . So why shouldn't he stay?
Blub . . . *blub* . . .

> Your friend,
> *Blub* . . . *blub* . . . *blub* . . .
> BUBBLES

FROM THE DESK OF

Simon

Dear Bubbles,

    I appreciate your forgiveness. Please understand that I am worried about you. You say the beast cannot reach your bowl, but beasts do tend to grow. And unlike cats, many of them enjoy playing in water. That could end badly for you.

With concern,

S-I-M-O-N

Dear Simon,

I'm not worried. Blub . . . blub . . . I like Baxter. Blub . . . blub . . . He's funny! Did you know he chases his own tail? Blub . . . blub . . . He can catch it, too! Have you ever tried chasing your tail? Blub . . . blub . . . No matter how hard I try, I can't seem to catch mine.

Your friend,
BUBBLES

SEVEN
NOT MY FAULT

Deer Simen,

I hope you get this letter befor you see Andy. I want you to noe that whut happend was not my fawlt. Andy was climing a tree and . . . he fell.

But gess whut? He climed a tree! YAY!!!!! I don't think he'd ever dun that befor.

Luv and Liver Treets,
Bax

FTS: Take good care of our boy. He needs a little extra luving rite now.

Simon

Dear Beast,

He fell? That's all you've got to say? Andy didn't just fall. He broke his arm!

I heard he was playing ball with you, the ball got stuck in a tree, he climbed up to get it, and he fell. How is that not your fault, Beast? You missed the ball! You let him climb the tree. And you failed to catch him when he fell.

It's your fault Andy got sick, your fault he didn't do his homework, and your fault he broke his arm. You are bad, bad, BAD for Andy, Beast! You need to leave. Now! Before things get even worse.

With clenched teeth,
SIMON

Blub . . .

Blub . . .

Dear Simon,
    Andy and his dad are so sad.
They miss Baxter. You know it's
your fault he left, right? I hope
you're happy. *Blub . . . blub . . .*

                NOT your friend,
                BUBBLES

FROM THE DESK OF
Simon

Dear Bubbles,

   I agree that Andy has been a bit unsettled by the beast's departure. But he'll snap out of it. Isn't it nicer at your house without the beast?

Warmly,
SIMON

Blub . . .

Blub . . .

Dear Simon,

I don't know if Andy will snap out of it.
He's very, Very, VERY sad! *Blub-BLUB . . .*

And no! The house is not nicer without
Baxter. *Blub-BLUB . . .* Andy and his dad are
so upset they keep forgetting to feed me!
I haven't had a meal in three days!!!
BLUB-BLUB . . .

Breathe and forgive. *Blub-BLUB . . .*

Breathe and forgive. *Blub-BLUB . . .*

Nope. I don't think I can do it this time.
Blub-BLUB . . .

And I don't think Andy will forgive you,
either. Do you enjoy seeing him so unhappy?
Blub-BLUB . . .

BUBBLES

FROM THE DESK OF
Simon

Dear Bubbles,

Of course I don't like it when Andy is unhappy. But the beast is gone. Can't we all move on?

Sincerely yours,
SIMON

Blub . . .

Blub . . .

Dear Simon,

If you want to "move on," here is what you need to do: blub . . . BLUB . . .

1. Find Baxter.
2. Say you're sorry.
3. Get him to come home.

Blub . . . BLUB . . . Just be a good pet, Simon! It's not that hard.

BUBBLES

TO WHOM IT MAY CONCERN

FROM THE DESK OF

Simon

To Whom It May Concern,

I'm looking for a lost dog. His name is Baxter. He was last seen jumping the fence at 123 Lake Park Lane. He cannot spell. He may have trouble catching balls.

If you've seen him, please write back.

Sincerely,
SIMON, the Cat

Dear Simon,

I know the dog you're talking about. He chased me out of his yard once. Maybe more than once.

I haven't seen him. But I've still got one of his liver treats! I'm saving it for a rainy day. Hahahahaha!!!!

Best,
    CHEEKS, the Squirrel

DEAR SIMON,

    I SAW BAXTER. HE WAS HANGING OUT BEHIND THE PIZZA PALACE A COUPLE DAYS AGO. HE DIDN'T UNDERSTAND THAT THAT'S MY TURF. MY TURF, SI! AND THAT WAS MY PIZZA CRUST HE STOLE. MOST OF US DON'T HAVE HUMANS TO BRING US FOOD ON A SILVER PLATTER, YOU KNOW. I DON'T KNOW WHERE HE WENT AFTER I CHASED HIM AWAY. DON'T CARE, EITHER.

                KIND REGARDS,
                TOM, THE CAT

Dear Simon,

   We know Baxter. We see him at the ballpark with his boy and our girl. Are you really trying to find him? We heard you're the one who made him leave. That concerns us.

   So if we have seen him, we aren't going to tell you. Others may feel the same way. Just saying. . . .

                    Loyally,
                       The Terrier Twins

Dear Simon,

   If I tell you where the dog is, do I get a reward?

                            Signed,
                               EDGAR ALLAN CROW

FROM THE DESK OF
Simon

Dear Edgar Allan Crow,
   Do you know where Baxter is???

                               Sincerely yours,
                               SIMON

Dear Simon,
    Maybe. I don't talk till I see the reward. The shinier it is, the more I'll say.
                    Signed,
                        EDGAR ALLAN CROW

Dear Simon,
    Well, that is a fine reward. A fine reward indeed.
    Yes, I know where the dog is. Unfortunately, he does not wish to be found. And his reward was shinier than yours. Sorry.

                    Signed,
                        EDGAR ALLAN CROW

FROM THE DESK OF
Simon

Dear Edgar Allan Crow,

FROM THE DESK OF
Simon

Dear Edgar Allan Crow,
   If you cannot tell me where Baxter is, can you ask him to please get in touch with me? Tell him I have news about our boy.

Sincerely,
SIMON

FINDING BEAST

Dear Simon,
  you have news about Andy???
What is it???
          Love and Liver Treats,
                Baxter

P.S. Edgar Allan Crow said you
called him "our" boy. YAY!!!!

FROM THE DESK OF

Simon

Dear Baxter,

Wow! There wasn't a single misspelling in your letter! I'm impressed.

Yes, I have news about Andy. He misses you. Furthermore, Andy's dad misses you. Even Bubbles misses you. Please return to 123 Lake Park Lane as soon as you can.

I am . . . sorry I asked you to leave.

Sincerely yours,
SIMON

Dear Simon,
   I told you I'm working on
my speling.
   Okay, I'll come back.

          Love and Liver Treats,
          Baxter

   FTS: Did you miss me?

Simon

Dear Baxter,

Andy is very busy going back and forth between his parents every other day. He also has school, friends, and now baseball, too. It is possible he does require the services of two pets after all. Therefore, I am suggesting we share this boy. What do you say?

Sincerely yours,
SIMON

Dear Simon,

I say: YAY!!!! But Simon, Andy has three pets, not two. You, me, and Bubbles! Don't ferget Bubbles! Isn't it funny that I have trubble speling and you have trubble cownting?

Anyway, you didn't anser my questchun. Did you miss me?

Love and Liver Treats,
Baxter

Simon

Dear Baxter,

My counting is just fine.

Sincerely,
SIMON

Dear Simon,

I missed you, too. Also, I think you shud call me Beast. It's sort of our thing.

Love and Liver Treats,
Beast

DOGGY DICTIONARY

abowt = about

adoptid = adopted

alreddy = already

anser = answer

anuther = another

arownd = around

bearly = barely

beest = beast

befor = before

biskit = biscuit

bizzy = busy

bord = board

brake = break

climed = climbed

climing = climbing

cownting = counting

cupple = couple

cuz = because

danse = dance

deel = deal

deer = dear

docktur = doctor

doo = due

dun = done

duz = does

duzn't = doesn't

enyway = anyway

evry = every

evrywon = everyone

fawlt = fault

ferget = forget

fergot = forgot

figyor = figure

fownd = found

frends = friends

FTS = Forgot to Say

gess = guess

grate = great

happend = happened

hay = hey

homewurk = homework

howse = house

hyooman = human

imbarrassed = embarrassed

importint = important

intire = entire

intresting = interesting

joose = juice

laffed = laughed

luv = love

luving = loving

meens = means

nick name = nickname

noe = know

nooz = news

owers = hours

owt = out

owtside = outside

pickchur = picture

plase = place

pleshur = pleasure

probly = probably

PS = P.S.

purson = person

questchun = question

ree-spon-su-bill-it-ee =
    responsibility

reelly = really

reeport = report

rite = write or right

ritten = written

rools = rules

sed = said

sens = sense
sez = says
shud = should
speek = speak
speling = spelling
sumthing = something
sumtimes = sometimes

tawt = taught
teech = teach
thay = they
thay're = they're
thro = throw
toematoe = tomato
towul = towel
treets = treats
trubble = trouble
tumorow = tomorrow

undrstud = understood

wantid = wanted
whut = what
wile = while
wood = would
wurk = work
wurking = working
wurry = worry

yestrday = yesterday
yoozing = using
yor = you're
yur = your

WHAT'S NEXT FOR
SIMON AND BAXTER? FIND OUT IN
DEAR BEAST: THE PET PARADE

IT'S TIME FOR THE ANNUAL CITY PET PARADE!

Simon has always hated wearing costumes, so he decides it's okay for Baxter to march with Andy instead. But when Baxter refuses to tell Simon about their costume, Simon changes his mind. Andy needs him. That beast can't be trusted—and it's up to Simon to save the day.